Dear Parents and Educators,

Welcome to Penguin Young Readers! As parents and educators, you know that each child develops at his or her own pace—in terms of speech, critical thinking, and, of course, reading. Penguin Young Readers recognizes this fact. As a result, each Penguin Young Readers book is assigned a traditional easy-to-read level (1–4) as well as a Guided Reading Level (A–P). Both of these systems will help you choose the right book for your child. Please refer to the back of each book for specific leveling information. Penguin Young Readers features esteemed authors and illustrators, stories about favorite characters, fascinating nonfiction, and more!

We Are Twins

LEVEL 1

GUIDED READING LEVEL **D**

This book is perfect for an **Emergent Reader** who:
- can read in a left-to-right and top-to-bottom progression;
- can recognize some beginning and ending letter sounds;
- can use picture clues to help tell the story; and
- can understand the basic plot and sequence of simple stories.

Here are some **activities** you can do during and after reading this book:
- Compare/Contrast: The narrator of this story tells her twin sister that "a lot is the same. But a lot is not." Discuss what she means by this. Then on a separate sheet of paper, make a list of how the twins are alike and how they are different.
- Rhyming Words: On a separate sheet of paper, make a list of all the rhyming words in this story. For example, *spot* rhymes with *not*, so write those words next to each other. Then come up with another word that rhymes with them. For example, *hot* rhymes with *spot* and *not*.

Remember, sharing the love of reading with a child is the best gift you can give!

—Bonnie Bader, EdM
  Penguin Young Readers program

D0207960

*Penguin Young Readers are leveled by independent reviewers applying the standards developed by Irene Fountas and Gay Su Pinnell in *Matching Books to Readers: Using Leveled Books in Guided Reading*, Heinemann, 1999.

For Mom and Ro, my favorite twins—LD

For Max and Colin—PC

Penguin Young Readers
Published by the Penguin Group
Penguin Group (USA) Inc., 375 Hudson Street, New York, New York 10014, USA
Penguin Group (Canada), 90 Eglinton Avenue East, Suite 700, Toronto, Ontario M4P 2Y3, Canada
(a division of Pearson Penguin Canada Inc.)
Penguin Books Ltd., 80 Strand, London WC2R 0RL, England
Penguin Group Ireland, 25 St. Stephen's Green, Dublin 2, Ireland (a division of Penguin Books Ltd.)
Penguin Group (Australia), 250 Camberwell Road, Camberwell, Victoria 3124, Australia
(a division of Pearson Australia Group Pty. Ltd.)
Penguin Books India Pvt. Ltd., 11 Community Centre, Panchsheel Park, New Delhi—110 017, India
Penguin Group (NZ), 67 Apollo Drive, Rosedale, Auckland 0632, New Zealand
(a division of Pearson New Zealand Ltd.)
Penguin Books (South Africa) (Pty.) Ltd., 24 Sturdee Avenue,
Rosebank, Johannesburg 2196, South Africa

Penguin Books Ltd., Registered Offices: 80 Strand, London WC2R 0RL, England

Text copyright © 2012 by Laura Driscoll. Illustrations copyright © 2012 by Penguin Group (USA) Inc.
All rights reserved. Published by Penguin Young Readers, an imprint of Penguin Group (USA) Inc.,
345 Hudson Street, New York, New York 10014. Manufactured in China.

Library of Congress Cataloging-in-Publication Data is available.

ISBN 978-0-448-46157-1   10 9 8 7 6 5 4 3 2 1

We Are Twins

by Laura Driscoll
illustrated by Pascal Campion

Penguin Young Readers
An Imprint of Penguin Group (USA) Inc.

We are twins.

One.

Two.

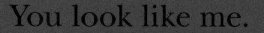

You look like me.

I look like you.

Same hair.

Same smile.

Same cheeks.

Same nose.

9

Same long fingers.

Same big toes.

Same tiny dot in

the very same spot.

A lot is the same.

But a lot is not.

I like soccer.

You like to dance.

I like dresses.

You like pants.

I play piano.

You play the drums.

You do not like bugs.

I think they are fun.

I swim and splash.

You sit and read.

I pick flowers.

You plant seeds.

I go slow.

You run, run, run.

But we both have fun, fun, fun.

I have wide eyes.

So do you.

But mine are brown.

Yours are blue.

And I am a little taller, too.

You look like me.

I look like you.

But I am me.

And you are you.

OTHER LEVEL 1 BOOKS

LOOK OUT FOR LEVEL 2 BOOKS

*Penguin Young Readers are leveled by independent reviewers applying the standards developed by Irene Fountas and Gay Su Pinnell in *Matching Books to Readers: Using Leveled Books in Guided Reading*, Heinemann, 1999.

We Are Twins

With twins, a lot **is** the same—but a lot is not! These little twin girls have the same hair and the same nose, but their eyes are different colors and they like different things, too. They are a very special set of twins!

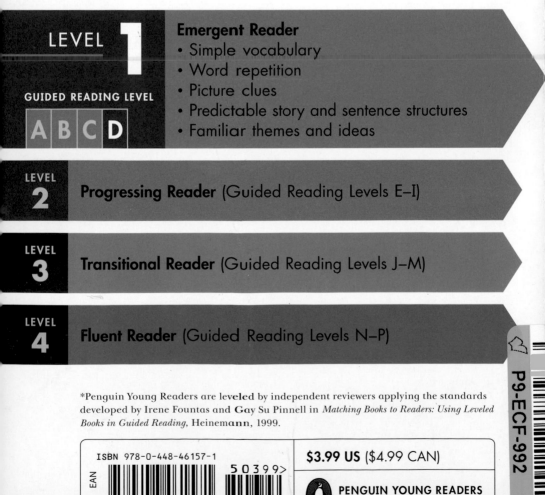

LEVEL 1

GUIDED READING LEVEL

A B C D

Emergent Reader
- Simple vocabulary
- Word repetition
- Picture clues
- Predictable story and sentence structures
- Familiar themes and ideas

LEVEL 2 **Progressing Reader** (Guided Reading Levels E–I)

LEVEL 3 **Transitional Reader** (Guided Reading Levels J–M)

LEVEL 4 **Fluent Reader** (Guided Reading Levels N–P)

*Penguin Young Readers are leveled by independent reviewers applying the standards developed by Irene Fountas and Gay Su Pinnell in *Matching Books to Readers: Using Leveled Books in Guided Reading*, Heinemann, 1999.

ISBN 978-0-448-46157-1

EAN

9 780448 461571

50399>

$3.99 US ($4.99 CAN)

PENGUIN YOUNG READERS
www.penguinyoungreaders.com

P9-ECF-992